Tracking the Gooey Clue

Freddie and Flossie headed down to the stream. Then they started walking slowly along the path that edged the water.

"Do you know what we're looking for?" Flossie asked.

"Not really," Freddie admitted. "Something a dog might eat that doesn't look as if it would be good for him."

Flossie sighed. "Chief will sniff almost anything he finds. But he hardly ever tries to eat it. How do you think he— Aieee!"

Flossie stepped on a patch of slippery mud. Her legs shot out from under her, and she fell at the edge of the path. Helplessly she slid down the short, steep bank.

A moment later, she hit the water with a loud splash!

Books in The New Bobbsey Twins™ Series

Available from MINSTREL Books

◆ THE NEW ◆

BOBBSEY

T?W◆I★N◆S ™

#26

The Clue at Casper Creek

LAURA LEE HOPE

Illustrated by DAVID F. HENDERSON

A MINSTREL® BOOK

PUBLISHED BY POCKET BOOKS

New York   London   Toronto   Sydney   Tokyo   Singapore

A MINSTREL PAPERBACK *ORIGINAL*

A Minstrel Book published by
POCKET BOOKS, a division of Simon & Schuster Inc.
1230 Avenue of the Americas, New York, NY 10020

Copyright © 1991 by Simon & Schuster Inc.
Cover art copyright © 1991 by Dominick Finelle
Produced by Mega-Books of New York, Inc.

ISBN: 0-671-73038-X

First Minstrel Books printing October 1991

10 9 8 7 6 5 4 3 2 1

The NEW BOBBSEY TWINS is a trademark of
Simon & Schuster Inc.

THE NEW BOBBSEY TWINS, A MINSTREL BOOK and colophon are registered trademarks of Simon & Schuster Inc.

Printed in the U.S.A.

Contents

The Clue
at Casper
Creek

1

Nothing but Trouble

"Hey, Nan!" Flossie Bobbsey called from the back door. "Why are you lying on the ground? I thought you were going to practice your gymnastics routine."

Flossie's twin brother, Freddie, joined her on the back porch of the Bobbsey house. "Maybe she got tired," he said.

"Nan? She *never* gets tired," Flossie teased.

The twins' twelve-year-old sister, Nan, stood up and brushed the grass off her sweatpants. "Every time I try to do a cartwheel," she said, "Chief knocks me over."

Flossie looked around the backyard. Chief, their sheepdog puppy, was near the garage. His eyes were fixed on a squirrel as his tail waved back and forth.

"Watch this," Nan said. She stretched her arms over her head and raised her left leg. Then she threw herself into a cartwheel.

Chief whipped around and ran toward Nan, barking loudly. Just as her feet touched the ground, he jumped. A moment later Nan was sprawled on her back again. Chief lowered his head and started licking her face.

"Will somebody come and get this stupid dog?" Nan complained. "How am I supposed to practice my routine with a half-witted bowwow on top of me?"

Flossie giggled and ran down the steps to the yard, her blond curls bouncing. She found Chief's collar under all his fur and tugged. Chief looked up with a hurt expression. He seemed to be saying, "What's wrong? I was only playing!"

While Flossie held the dog, Nan got up and brushed herself off again. "You guys look like you're going somewhere," she said. "What's up?"

"We're on litter patrol this morning," Flossie replied.

Freddie walked over to his sisters. "Our school is taking part in the Clean Up Casper Creek campaign," he explained. "Each class covers a different part of the stream. We pick up litter, study the plants and animals—stuff like that."

Nan nodded. "You know," she said, "you two have taken on a pretty hard job. I think you're going to need help."

"Well, if you really want—" Freddie began.

Nan cut him off. "What you need," she said with a grin, "is a well-trained dog who can sniff out garbage. Sheepdogs are very good at that."

"No way," said Flossie. "We won't get anything done if Chief's along."

Chief seemed to know they were talking about him. He crouched down and started to whine softly.

"Oh, all right," Flossie said with a sigh. She knelt down and gave Chief a hug. "I was just kidding. We'll take you with us."

Chief stood up suddenly, and Flossie fell over backward.

Freddie and Nan started to laugh.

Flossie sat up. "It's not funny," she said. "I think we're making a big mistake."

While Chief galloped around the yard, chasing an orange-and-black butterfly, Freddie ran to get trash bags from the garage. Then the twins set off to meet some other kids from their class.

The walk to Casper Creek usually took about ten minutes. But this time, after ten minutes, Flossie and Freddie were still only two blocks from home. Chief was playing hide-and-seek in Mrs. Bover's tulip beds.

"Here, boy!" Freddie called from the sidewalk. He waved the pup's leash. "Come on, Chief. Good dog."

Flossie placed her hands on her hips. "What do you mean, 'good dog'?" she demanded.

Chief gave a playful yelp and came bounding across the Bovers' yard. Flossie dodged his muddy paws. "You have to learn to listen!" she told him sternly.

Chief looked up with his tongue hanging out. His tail started to wag. Then he spotted a cat down the block. A moment later, he took off after it.

Flossie looked at Freddie and frowned. "We'd better catch up to him," she said, "before he gets into trouble."

But by the time they reached the end of the block, Chief had run off somewhere else. Freddie tried calling, "Chief! Here, boy!" a few times. Then he gave up.

"We should have kept him on his leash," Flossie said.

Freddie nodded. "I guess you're right," he said. "But we have to teach Chief to obey us."

Flossie rolled her eyes. "Forget it," she said.

"Let's just go ahead," Freddie told his twin. "This time Chief can find *us*."

The twins had nearly reached Casper Creek when they heard a furious burst of barking. It was coming from inside the chain-link fence surrounding the Lakeport Marina.

"That sounds like Chief," said Flossie. "He's in trouble!"

The twins ran to the gate of the marina. Just inside was a half-painted boat resting on a trailer. Near it was Chief. He was crouched low to the ground, a paintbrush in his mouth.

"Nice doggy," a man in paint-spattered overalls was saying. "Give it here, doggy."

He walked slowly toward Chief, holding out his hand. Chief backed up, just as slowly. He knew this game.

The man snatched at the paintbrush. Chief sprang out of reach, then waited, tail wagging.

"Chief!" Freddie shouted. "Drop it!"

The sheepdog looked over at the twins.

Then he dropped the paintbrush and trotted over to them. He looked very pleased with himself.

"Is that your dog?" the man demanded. "You'd better keep him out of this marina from now on. He could get into a lot of trouble."

"Sorry," Freddie said. "He won't do it again."

The man shook his head angrily. Then he walked over to pick up his paintbrush.

Back on the street, Flossie said, "We'll never get our cleanup done if Chief keeps this up." She grabbed Chief by the collar. "Home, boy," Flossie said sternly. "Go home!"

Tail drooping, the pup turned and slunk away.

"Do you think it'll work?" asked Freddie.

Flossie shrugged. "He's going in the right direction, anyway. Come on, let's get to the stream. Ms. Hanson and the other kids must be there already."

Ms. Hanson was Flossie and Freddie's

teacher. She was the one who had helped the kids at Lakeport Elementary organize the Clean Up Casper Creek campaign.

Half an hour later, the twins and some of their classmates had filled six plastic bags with old cans, bottles, fast-food boxes, and scraps of paper. As they worked, they sorted the litter for recycling.

"Why can't people put trash where it belongs?" Flossie complained. She pushed one of the bags with her toe. "The creek could be really beautiful without all this junk lying around."

"It will be, when we're done," Freddie said. He took off his rubber gloves. "Come on, let's turn our bags over to Ms. Hanson and go home. We can take the shortcut through the woods."

They found Ms. Hanson a short way up the creek with two other kids from the cleanup team. Flossie and Freddie gave her their sacks of litter and said goodbye. Then they climbed the bank and started along the narrow path.

Flossie scuffed her shoes through the dead leaves on the path, pretending to ice-skate.

Suddenly Freddie grabbed her arm. "Shh!" he whispered. "Listen!"

Flossie stood still and held her breath. There was a rustling of leaves from somewhere inside the woods.

Now the sound was drawing closer.

Something was stalking them!

2

Riding Toward Disaster

"It sounds big," Flossie whispered, as the noise came even closer. "Do you think it's a bear?"

"Don't be silly. There aren't any bears in Lakeport," Freddie whispered back. "At least, I don't think so."

"Maybe we should run," said Flossie. Freddie nodded. "Ready? One, two— Yikes!"

A large, dark form jumped out of the bushes, straight at Flossie. As she fell backward on the path, she scrunched her eyes closed.

Whatever was about to happen, she didn't want to see it.

Suddenly she felt a big, wet tongue licking her cheek. She opened her eyes.

"Chief!" Flossie exclaimed. "Why aren't you at home?"

She pushed him away and stood up. "Yuck," she said. "You're all wet and muddy, and you smell terrible!"

The sheepdog gave her a hurt look. Then he whirled around and jumped up on Freddie.

"Hey, get down!" Freddie shouted. He pushed at Chief's chest. "Cut it out!"

Flossie started to laugh. Freddie now had two perfect paw prints on the front of his T-shirt. Then she glanced down at her jeans and stopped laughing. They were streaked with black, gooey stains.

Chief turned back to Flossie, ready to play some more. She grabbed his collar with both hands and took a deep breath. "You—you—" she began. Then she sighed. "Oh, never mind.

You didn't know any better, you silly dog. Let's get you home and give you a good bath."

Chief let out a loud bark. Freddie sneaked up on him and fastened the leash to his collar. Then the twins walked him home.

When they arrived, Flossie tied Chief to a tree in the backyard. Then she hooked up the garden hose. Freddie brought a big metal washtub from the basement.

The minute Chief saw the washtub, he started barking frantically. Nan and Bert came rushing out of the house to see what was the matter. Bert was Nan's twin.

"Boy, that dog is a mess," said Bert. "What did he get into?"

"Who knows?" Freddie replied. "Want to help us clean him up?"

"No, thanks," Bert said. He backed toward the door.

Nan glared at him. "We'll help," she said.

Bert held up his hands. "Okay, okay."

Freddie turned on the water and started to

fill the tub. Flossie ran inside to get the dog shampoo. Nan and Bert untied Chief, took him by the collar, and urged him over to the tub.

Chief went along peacefully until he saw the water. Then he dug his front paws into the grass and refused to budge.

"Don't expect me to carry him," said Bert. "I don't want that gunk all over me."

"I'll do it," Flossie said. "I'm already so dirty that it doesn't matter."

She bent down and picked up Chief's leash. He took a leap to one side, dragging Flossie with him. Her left foot got caught in a loop of the garden hose. The nozzle flipped out of the washtub, and the stream of water hit Bert.

"Turn it off!" Bert sputtered, wiping his face.

"At least the water's clean," Nan teased.

"Chief!" Flossie shouted. "Come back here!"

The sheepdog vanished around the corner

of the house. He was heading for the street. Flossie ran after him.

"I'll go the other way and cut him off," Freddie called.

Chief was loping down the driveway now. Flossie hoped he would remember not to run into the street. "Chief!" she called again. "Stop! Come back!"

Just as the pup reached the sidewalk, a bicycle came speeding up. Chief swerved one way, and the cyclist swerved the other. The bicycle and its rider ended up in the bushes near the Bobbseys' front walk. Chief trotted over to investigate.

"Are you all right?" Flossie cried. She ran toward the fallen bike. "I'm sorry, our dog—"

She skidded to a halt. Danny Rugg, the biggest bully in Lakeport, was climbing out of the bushes. Danny's favorite hobby was picking on the younger Bobbsey twins.

"You just wait," Danny said, scowling. "I'm going to make you pay for this. You and that stupid mutt of yours."

Flossie backed up as Danny came toward her. But just then, Freddie came running toward them. At the same time, Nan and Bert appeared from the other direction.

Outnumbered, Danny muttered a few more threats. Then he picked up his bike, checked it for damage, and rode off.

"We're in trouble now, Chief," Flossie said. The twins dragged the puppy back to the washtub for his bath. "Why did you have to mess with Danny Rugg?"

That night after supper, the Bobbseys were watching TV when Flossie heard a strange sound. It seemed to be coming from the backyard. Was it the wind? She went to the back door and listened. No. She turned on the porch light and stepped outside to investigate.

Moments later, she dashed back into the living room. "Come quick, everybody!" she said urgently. "There's something wrong with Chief! He's whimpering, and he can't stand up. I think he's really sick!"

3

One Sorry Dog

Dr. Morrison, the veterinarian, stood up and closed her bag. "Chief is a very sick dog," she said. "But I'm sure he'll be all right. Just keep him warm and let him sleep. Then bring him in to my office on Monday so I can take another look at him."

"But what's wrong with Chief?" asked Freddie. He was kneeling next to the basket, stroking the sheepdog's head.

"I can't be certain," the vet replied. "But Chief must have run into something poisonous."

"Poisonous?" cried Nan.

Dr. Morrison nodded. "It looks that way."

"That's pretty mean," Bert said. "Who would give our dog something bad for him?"

"Whoa," the vet said, holding up her hand. "I didn't say it was done on purpose. I doubt that. But Chief did come across something harmful somewhere. That's my guess, anyway. Now you'll just have to keep him comfortable until he feels better."

"We've got to find out what that stuff was," said Freddie. "If we don't, Chief might go back later and eat more of it."

Flossie nodded. "Besides, someone else's pet might find it and get sick. Wild animals, too. Remember what Ms. Hanson said, about how everything in nature is part of a chain?"

"That's a good point, Flossie," said Dr. Morrison. She smiled and walked to the door. "Good night, everybody, and good luck with your search. Call me if I can be of any help."

* * *.

The next morning, when Freddie came downstairs, Chief raised his head off his blanket and wagged his tail. But he didn't try to stand up. Freddie knelt down and scratched him behind the ears.

Flossie came into the living room a few minutes later. "Chief's feeling better, isn't he?"

"I think so," Freddie replied. "But he's still pretty sick. I hope we can find the stuff that did this to him."

"Maybe we should go around and talk to people in the neighborhood," Flossie said. "Somebody may have noticed something."

Freddie nodded. "Okay," he said. "Let's go."

"*After* breakfast," Mr. Bobbsey called from the kitchen. "I'm not going to eat all these pancakes by myself."

"Don't worry, Dad," Freddie said eagerly. "I'm starving."

He and Flossie went into the kitchen and

started setting the table. When Nan and Bert appeared, Freddie told them their plan.

Bert began to pour the orange juice. "I'd help you guys," he said, "but I have to go over to Charlie Mason's today to work on a project for school."

"And I have a gymnastics lesson," Nan said. "But I'll be home at one o'clock. I can stay with Chief this afternoon."

Flossie jumped up from her chair and ran back to the living room. "Don't worry, boy." Flossie patted Chief on the head. "You're going to get better, and we're going to find out what made you so sick. That's a promise."

Chief just looked up at her with big, sad eyes.

"I don't think we're *ever* going to solve this," Freddie told Flossie two hours later. He kicked at a clump of dirt on the sidewalk.

"Why not?" demanded Flossie. She brushed her hair back and tucked it behind her ears. "Just about everybody we've talked to saw Chief yesterday."

Freddie snorted. "Sure they did," he said. "There's Mr. Lannom. Chief knocked over his birdbath. And the Schicks. Chief treed a squirrel in their yard. He barked so loudly that Alice couldn't practice her piano lesson."

"Don't forget Mrs. Velez," Flossie said with a giggle. "She caught Chief trying to get into her baby's playpen."

"Chief loves babies," Freddie protested. "I bet he was just standing there with his front paws up on the rail."

Then Freddie looked down and started to draw a design in the dirt with the toe of his sneaker. "I'm sorry Chief got into so much trouble," he said. "But the main thing is, we still don't have a clue about what made him sick."

"Nobody saw him eat anything," said Flossie. "And if there *was* anything dangerous lying around where Chief could get to it, nobody admitted it. But we can't give up now.

There are lots of people we haven't questioned yet."

She glanced around. "Look, there's Ms. Forman, working in her flower bed," she said. "She's always liked Chief. Maybe she noticed something."

Ms. Forman saw them coming and straightened up. "I hope you don't have that puppy of yours with you," she called. "He may be cute, but my irises can't take much more trampling."

Freddie noticed that the stems of some of the plants in the flower bed were broken. "Did Chief do that?" he asked.

"He certainly did," Ms. Forman said. "I guess he was in a hurry to get somewhere."

"We're really sorry," said Flossie.

Ms. Forman took a new flower bulb from a wooden box on the ground next to her. She placed it in a small hole she had dug. Then she carefully patted earth around it. "I don't mind so much," she said. "He's just a high-spirited animal, I guess."

"Chief's spirits aren't very high today," Freddie said. "He got really sick last night. The vet says it's something he ate, and we're trying to find out what. Did he eat anything here?"

"No, not that I saw." Ms. Forman rubbed her chin. "If he ate one of my iris bulbs, I don't suppose he'd like it very much, but I don't think it would make him sick. And it doesn't look as though he dug up any bulbs. He just ran through the flowers a few times, that's all."

Freddie took a deep breath. He and Flossie were doing a lot of apologizing for Chief this morning. But as he opened his mouth, someone shoved him from behind.

Freddie stumbled forward, and his left foot caught on the brick border of the flower bed. Freddie fell headfirst, right onto the irises Ms. Forman had just planted.

4

Now There Are Two

"Oh, no!" Ms. Forman cried. "Are you all right? What happened? Did you lose your balance?"

"I don't know," Freddie replied. He struggled to his feet and looked around. "Somebody pushed me."

"It was Danny Rugg!" Flossie cried. "That big bully!"

Freddie was a mess. Mud caked his hands and the knees of his jeans. He had a green stain on his cheek from one of the plants.

Down the block, Danny was watching the twins from his bike. He was laughing.

"He pushed you while he was riding by," Flossie said angrily. She frowned. "Uh-oh, here he comes again."

Danny was riding right down the middle of the sidewalk, straight at them. Quickly Flossie and Freddie stepped onto the grass. But before Danny reached them, Ms. Forman stood up.

"Danny Rugg!" she called. "You should be ashamed, picking on children smaller than you. I've a good mind to call your mother and tell her the way you've been acting."

Danny skidded to a halt. "Sorry, Ms. Forman," he said. "It was just an accident," he added with a smirk.

Then he gave Flossie and Freddie an evil look. "Hey, squirts," he said. "I hear that mutt of yours is real sick. That's too bad!" Laughing, he wheeled his bike around and sped down the street.

Ms. Forman shook her head and returned to her flowers.

"Thanks for your help, Ms. Forman," Flossie said.

"You're welcome," their neighbor replied. "I hope your dog feels better soon."

"Freddie, did you hear what Danny said?" Flossie asked as they walked away.

Freddie brushed at the dirt on his jeans. "Sure," he replied. "Some accident!"

"I don't mean that," said Flossie. "I mean about Chief. How did Danny find out that Chief's sick?"

"We've told a lot of people this morning," Freddie pointed out. "Maybe one of them told him."

"Maybe." Flossie hesitated. "But maybe he already knew. Remember yesterday, when Danny told us we were going to be sorry and so was Chief? Well, Chief got sick right after that."

Freddie stopped and stared at his twin. "You don't really think Danny gave Chief something that made him sick, do you?" he asked.

"I don't know," Flossie said slowly. "I guess it's kind of hard to believe that even Danny would do something that mean. But he could have."

"That doesn't sound like Danny," Freddie said. He shook his head. "If people found out he'd done something like that, nobody would ever speak to him again. He's too much of a coward to take that kind of chance."

"Unless he was sure nobody would find out," Flossie said. "Oh, well, come on. Let's try the next block. Maybe somebody there saw something."

Halfway down the block, a man was trimming his hedges. The twins asked him if he'd seen a sheepdog the day before. His face hardened.

"Why? Was that your dog?" he asked.

"Yes, it was," Freddie replied.

"Wait right here," the man said. "I want to show you something." He went into the house and came out again a few moments later. In his hand was a folded bed sheet. He grabbed the corners and unfurled it.

"What do you have to say about this?" he demanded.

Flossie wished the ground would open and let her drop right out of sight. There were half a dozen rips along one edge of the sheet. And the muddy paw prints all over it couldn't be mistaken.

"Did Chief do this?" she asked in a small voice.

"He certainly did," the man replied. "This sheet was hanging up to dry in the backyard. That pooch of yours jumped at it until he pulled it off the line. Then he ran all over it. My wife had a fit when she saw this sheet."

"We're really sorry, mister," said Freddie.

Flossie was about to ask the man if he'd seen Chief eat anything when a teenager in a blue satin baseball jacket walked up to them.

"Hi," the teenager said. "Are you the kids whose dog got sick yesterday?"

"That's right," Freddie replied. "Why? Do you know something about it?"

The man they had been talking to refolded his sheet and took it back into his house.

"Maybe I do," the teenager replied. "My name's Eric Windemann. We live over on Jackson Street. This morning, Kelly, my Irish setter, was really sick. We took him to see Dr. Morrison. She said she thought Kelly had the same thing as the Bobbseys' dog."

"Really?" said Freddie, frowning.

Eric nodded. "Uh-huh. I went by your house just now. Your dad told me you were going around the neighborhood, asking people if they knew anything. So I came looking for you. I figured I could save you some trouble."

"You mean, you know what happened to our dogs?" Flossie asked.

"I've got a pretty good hunch," Eric replied. "You know Mrs. Walters, a couple of blocks down?"

"You mean the cat lady?" Freddie said.

"Sure, everybody knows about her. She must have about a zillion cats in her house."

"That's right," said Eric. "And some of those cats are pretty mean, too. Kelly keeps getting into fights with them, and Mrs. Walters knows it. Well, last Friday I found Kelly in her yard. She was really mad. I said I was sorry and told her it wouldn't happen again. She gave me this crazy look and said she'd see that it didn't."

"Wow!" Flossie exclaimed. "That sounds like a threat."

"It sure did," Eric agreed. "And now, two days later, Kelly is sick. You know what I think? I think Mrs. Walters poisoned him. And I bet the old witch poisoned *your* dog, too!"

5

Revenge of the Cat Lady

"That's crazy!" exclaimed Freddie. "How could anybody poison a neighbor's dog?"

Eric shrugged. "I thought I should tell you," he said. "Look, I have to go home to take care of Kelly. And from now on, I'm going to make sure he stays far away from Mrs. Walters and her cats."

As the boy walked away, Freddie turned to his sister. "Do *you* think somebody poisoned Chief?"

"Well . . ." Flossie hesitated. "A few minutes ago I thought maybe Danny Rugg had.

Now I just don't know. We'd better check out Mrs. Walters, though. If she's as nutty as Eric thinks, she might do anything."

Mrs. Walters's house was easy to spot. A big black cat with white mittens was stretched out across the front walk. The twins stepped over the cat and walked toward the house. From the bushes, an orange tabby and a gray long-haired cat watched them come closer. Then the two cats faded into the leaves.

Freddie raised the door knocker and let it fall. No one answered.

"Try again," Flossie said. She went back down the steps and looked at the front of the house. From a window on the right, three more cats stared at her. There were no other signs of life.

"I don't think Mrs. Walters is home," said Freddie. He joined Flossie on the walk. "Let's try talking to some of her neighbors. We can come back here later."

"Okay," Flossie replied quickly. As she

turned toward the street, she was sure all those cats were watching her.

The woman who lived to the left of Mrs. Walters had been away the day before and hadn't seen anything. At the house on the right, though, Flossie and Freddie had better luck.

"A gray-and-white sheepdog, about so high?" asked the man who came to the door. "Sure, I saw him. Why? Is he lost?"

"No, but he got sick last night," Freddie explained. "We thought he might have eaten something bad for him."

"Well, he seemed pretty chipper when I saw him," the man said with a chuckle. "I was sitting in the backyard with the newspaper and a glass of iced tea. He came over to make friends, I guess. Nice dog, but he's too big to be climbing on people's laps."

"Did you notice which direction he came from?" Flossie asked eagerly.

The man's eyebrows drew together. "Not

exactly," he said. "He might have come from next door."

"From Mrs. Walters's house, you mean?" Freddie asked.

"That's right," the man said, nodding. "There was a lot of barking at one point. I remember thinking that some dog must be tangling with those cats of hers. Then your sheepdog came trotting into my yard, so it must have been him I heard. But why don't you ask Mrs. Walters? She keeps a close eye on what happens around her house."

"We knocked at her door," said Freddie. "But no one answered."

"Did you ring the bell?" the man asked. "Her hearing isn't what it used to be. She has a flashing light rigged up to the doorbell. It lets her know when someone's ringing. You ought to try again. She's usually home this time of day."

"Thanks," Flossie said. "We will." She shivered, thinking again of all those cats.

Back at Mrs. Walters's house, the twins saw that the black cat was still asleep on the walk. But now there were four or five cats watching from the bushes, instead of two. One of them, skinny and gray with a striped tail, came out and rubbed against Flossie's leg. But when she reached down to stroke it, it jumped away.

Freddie found the bell and pushed it. A few moments later, Flossie heard footsteps coming toward the door. The door swung open.

"Yes? What is it?"

Mrs. Walters was tall and thin, with wavy gray hair. "Have you come about the kittens?" she asked. "I'm sorry, but I've decided to keep the rest of them myself."

"It's not that," Freddie said nervously. "We were wondering if you saw our dog yesterday."

"He's a sheepdog puppy," Flossie added. "He's mostly dark gray and white, about this high." She held her hand just below her waist.

"No, I'm afraid not," Mrs. Walters said. "Now, if you'll excuse me . . ."

She started to close the door.

Freddie thought fast. "We were afraid he might have bothered your cats," he said quickly. "He's very friendly, but he's not used to being around cats."

Mrs. Walters shook her head. "No, I'm afraid not," she said again.

Flossie stepped forward. "But your next-door neighbor heard Chief barking in your yard," she said. "Are you sure—"

"Your dog wasn't here," Mrs. Walters said, and she shut the door.

As they went down the walk, Flossie said, "I just know that lady's hiding something. She didn't even want to talk to us."

"Maybe she doesn't like kids, only cats," Freddie suggested.

"Maybe," said Flossie. "But I'll bet—"

"Look!" Freddie interrupted. He pointed at the ground. "There, in the mud by the bushes. What do those look like to you?"

Flossie squatted down and peered at the paw

prints in the mud. "They're just like the ones Chief left on your T-shirt," she said. "That proves it. He *was* here yesterday. Mrs. Walters must have been lying to us."

"I guess you're right," said Freddie. "So what is Mrs. Walters trying to hide?"

6

Hiding Out

"Come on," Freddie said, tugging at Flossie's arm. "The cat lady might be watching us from the house. Let's go where she can't see us."

"Okay," Flossie agreed quickly. "This place gives me the creeps, anyway."

But when they were halfway down the block, Freddie said, "We'd better go back there and hide so we can watch Mrs. Walters's house."

"Do we have to?" Flossie said, frowning.

"She gave Chief something that made him sick, remember?" Freddie said. "Now she's afraid we'll find out she did it. That's why she tried to pretend that he wasn't in her yard yesterday."

"We don't know for sure that Chief was there," Flossie pointed out. "Just that he was in the bushes at the edge of her yard."

Freddie snorted. "If he wasn't, then Mrs. Walters's yard must have been the only one in Lakeport he *wasn't* in! Besides, the man next door heard barking just before Chief showed up. Look, it's obvious. Mrs. Walters hates dogs because she's crazy about cats. That's why she gave something to Chief and what's his name—"

"Kelly," Flossie said.

"Right, Kelly," Freddie agreed. "Anyway, it was something that made them both sick. She probably put out a dish of poisoned dog food. So we're going to hide and watch her house. Maybe we'll catch her trying to poison another dog. Then we'll make her stop, and Chief won't be in danger anymore. Okay?"

"Well . . ." Flossie hesitated. "Okay, I guess."

"Great. Let's go," said Freddie.

Three minutes later, Flossie was crawling on her hands and knees through the bushes in Mrs. Walters's backyard. She paused to untangle a twig that was yanking her hair. Freddie was just in front of her.

"I see a good spot," he whispered over his shoulder.

Flossie sighed. She was starting to be sorry that she had agreed to this plan. She was also starting to wonder if a spider was crawling down the back of her neck. Not that it mattered. A detective on a stakeout wasn't supposed to mind things like spiders.

Flossie crawled up next to Freddie. Through the leaves, she could see Mrs. Walters's backyard.

Two cats were sitting on the back steps. Three more were sunning themselves on the grass. Another, a Siamese, was walking slowly toward them. The dark tip of its tail waved slowly from side to side. Flossie was suddenly very glad that she wasn't a bird or a mouse.

"What am I supposed to be looking for?" she whispered to Freddie. "All I see is a bunch of cats."

"Right," he whispered back. "And no dogs!"

Flossie rolled her eyes. "Of course not. Mrs. Walters keeps cats."

"Right," Freddie said again. "But we know how she keeps the dogs away."

The minutes passed. Even the Siamese cat got bored and stalked away. Flossie began to study two lines of ants on the ground, a few inches from her face. One line was marching from right to left, the other from left to right.

A door slammed. Flossie and Freddie raised their heads and peered through the screen of leaves. Mrs. Walters was standing on her back steps. She had a food dish in each hand.

"Here, kitty, kitty, kitty," she called. Then

she placed the two dishes on the ground and went back inside. A moment later, she brought out two more dishes. Then she went back into the house.

From every side of the yard, cats began to appear. There were so many that Flossie gave up trying to count them. They crowded around the four food dishes.

"Are they all hers?" Flossie whispered.

Freddie shook his head. "A lot of them must be strays," he said. "Uh-oh—here comes trouble!"

A gold-colored spaniel had just wandered into the backyard. It hesitated for a moment, then headed for the nearest food dish. A big gray cat fixed its eyes on the dog, arched its back, and hissed. The spaniel stopped, crouched down, and started to bark.

The back door opened with a crash.

"Shoo! Scat!" Mrs. Walters shouted at the spaniel. "I've warned you for the last time!"

Flossie grabbed Freddie's arm and squeezed

it hard. She could barely keep herself from gasping out loud.

As the twins watched helplessly, Mrs. Walters raised a spray gun filled with bright green liquid. Then she pointed it straight at the spaniel!

7

Making a Splash

Mrs. Walters took careful aim and squeezed the trigger of the spray gun. A stream of the green liquid shot out and hit the spaniel's left ear. The dog let out a yelp, followed by several angry barks.

Mrs. Walters squeezed the trigger again. Her aim was a little off this time. The cats around the nearby food dish scattered as some of the spray hit them.

The next shot of spray sent the spaniel running, its tail between its legs.

"And don't come back!" Mrs. Walters

shouted. She put the spray bottle down on the steps. "There, there, kitties," she said in a very different voice. "Enjoy your lunch. That mean old dog won't bother you again." Then she turned and went back into the house.

Freddie started to get up. "Wait here," he whispered.

"What are you doing?" Flossie asked. But her brother was already racing across the yard, bent over in a crouch. He reached the steps, grabbed the spray bottle, and shot a stream of the liquid into his hand. Then he ran back to the hedge and dived for cover.

"Here, smell," he said, holding his hand out to Flossie.

She took a cautious sniff. "It smells like dishwashing soap," she said. "But weaker."

"That's what I thought, too," Freddie replied. He grabbed some leaves and wiped off his hand. "Come on, let's get out of here. Nan and Bert should be home by now. And I want to find out how Chief is doing."

* * *

"Dishwashing liquid?" Nan asked, as she set a tray of sandwiches on the table. "Would that make Chief really sick?"

Bert brought a pitcher of apple juice and a carton of milk from the refrigerator. "It might, if he drank it," he said. "But just getting sprayed with it wouldn't do much more than clean him off."

Freddie and Flossie finished setting four places. Their mother had a meeting that day, and their father was catching up on paperwork at the lumberyard he owned.

Freddie pulled out his chair and sat down. "How about this idea?" he said, reaching for a sandwich. "The spray is just for chasing dogs away. But if they don't *stay* away, Mrs. Walters puts out some food with poison in it. And that's what happened to Chief and Kelly."

"No way," said Flossie. "You saw what happened when she put those food dishes down. Every cat in the neighborhood showed up. She wouldn't run the risk of poisoning a kitty by mistake, would she?"

"Good point, Floss," Bert said. "And here's another one. Didn't you say that some of the spray hit her cats? She wouldn't have used that stuff around them if it was that harmful."

Freddie took a handful of corn chips out of a bowl. "Maybe you're right," he said. "Maybe she's just a nutty lady who wants to keep dogs away from her cats. But think about it. Chief and Eric's dog were both in her yard yesterday. Both of them got sick. And Dr. Morrison thought they had the same sickness. Do you really think that's a coincidence?"

"No," Flossie said. "But wait a minute. What if both Chief and Kelly were somewhere else, too? That could be where they ate the stuff that made them sick. We'd better talk to Eric again, right away!"

She bounced up out of her chair, but Nan caught her by the sleeve. "Hey, what about your lunch?" Nan said. "I thought you were starving."

"I'm done," Flossie said. "I'll go find Eric's address in the phone book." Freddie grabbed the rest of his sandwich and followed his twin out the kitchen door.

Eric was sitting on his front porch. Beside him was a big wicker basket. As Freddie and Flossie started up the steps, a feeble "woof!" came from inside the basket.

"Hi, Kelly," Freddie said. The dark red Irish setter raised his head and barked again. Then he lay down with closed eyes. "How's he doing?" Freddie asked Eric.

"Better," Eric replied with a shrug. "How about your dog?"

"Chief's better, too," said Flossie. "But we're still wondering what happened to him."

"Well, I already told you what I think," Eric said.

Freddie nodded. "I know," he said. "But could you tell us everywhere you went with Kelly yesterday?"

"I can try," the teenager said. "Let's see. We were home all morning. I was working on my

computer, and Kelly was in the backyard. Then, after lunch, we . . ."

Freddie took notes as Eric talked. When he had finished, the twins looked at each other.

"There's hardly any overlap," Flossie said. She picked up Freddie's notes and compared them with the list of Chief's movements that they had made before lunch.

"Wait a minute!" Flossie said excitedly. "Except for Mrs. Walters's backyard, the only place both dogs went was Casper Creek!"

"There must be something poisonous at the creek," Freddie said. "And we were too busy picking up litter to notice it!"

Flossie was already starting down the steps. "Thanks, Eric," Freddie called. "We'll let you know what we find."

This time, the walk past the marina to the mouth of the creek didn't take long at all. Freddie and Flossie headed down the slope to the bank of the stream. Then they started walking slowly along the path that edged the water.

"Do you know what we're looking for?" Flossie asked.

"Not really," Freddie admitted. "Something a dog might eat that looks as if it wouldn't be good for him."

Flossie sighed. "Chief will sniff almost anything he finds," she said, "but he hardly ever tries to eat it. How do you think he— Aieee!"

Flossie's left foot had landed on a patch of slippery mud. Her legs shot out from under her. She twisted, trying to land without hurting herself. Instead she fell at the edge of the path. Helplessly she slid down the short, steep bank.

A moment later she hit the water with a loud splash!

8

The Telltale Clue

"Hold on, Flossie!" shouted Freddie. "I'm coming!"

The water in Casper Creek didn't come much higher than Flossie's knees. But each time she tried to get to her feet, she slipped and fell again. Freddie grabbed a branch of a thick bush with one hand and crept as close to the edge of the muddy bank as he could. Then he stretched his other hand out to Flossie.

Suddenly Freddie's feet slid out from under him. A moment later one of his legs was in the creek, but he had kept his hold on the bush.

Using his other foot, he pushed himself up and managed to grip the branch with his free hand.

"Keep holding on," Flossie called. "I'll use your foot to help me out."

Freddie held on to the bush with all his strength. Flossie grabbed his ankle and pulled herself out of the stream. Moments later, the twins were both stretched out on the path above the creek, catching their breath.

"Whew!" Freddie said. "You smell as bad as Chief did yesterday." He got to his feet and pulled Flossie up.

"Thanks a lot," Flossie replied. She wrinkled her nose. "You smell even worse." Then Flossie looked down at the dark stains on her jeans and sneakers. "This gunk better wash out," she added. "It must be all over the creek bottom."

Freddie stared at the black goo on Flossie's jeans, then at his twin. "Chief!" he said. "I bet this is what made him sick!"

"You're right," said Flossie, frowning. "He

60

was covered with this stuff until we gave him that bath."

She looked down at the surface of Casper Creek. "The water looks so pretty and clear," she said. "Who'd ever think it really was polluted?"

"The gunk must have settled to the bottom and mixed with the mud," Freddie said. "That's why nobody noticed it.

"We'd better get home fast," he added. "If that stuff made Chief sick, who knows what it might do to you?"

When the twins reached home, Flossie immediately ran to take a shower. Freddie told Bert and Nan about their discovery.

"That means that the poison must have gotten into Chief through his skin," said Bert.

"Uh-huh," Freddie replied. "And that's why we couldn't figure out what he'd eaten that made him sick. It wasn't anything he ate, after all!"

Flossie stepped into the hallway. She was wearing a big bathrobe, and she had wrapped a towel around her head. "But what is that stuff?" she demanded. "And what are we going to do about it?"

"We'll have to report this to the State Environmental Protection Office first thing tomorrow morning," Bert said. "They can run tests on the creek and try to track down where the pollution came from."

"But that might take forever," Flossie protested. "Ms. Hanson told us that there are so many environmental problems that the government agencies can't handle them all. That's why our class started the Clean Up Casper Creek campaign."

"And that's what we're going to do," said Freddie. "We're going to clean up the creek! The first step is to track the pollution to its source."

Nan frowned. "That may not be easy," she said. "Lake Metoka flows into Casper Creek, you know. Anything that polluted the lake could end up in the creek."

"Yes, but—" Flossie began. Then she stopped in confusion.

"What is it?" Nan prompted.

"Well," Flossie said, frowning. "That gunk was on the creek bottom. So it must be heavy, right?"

Nan nodded. "That's right," she said. "That means it wouldn't travel very far. The pollution must be coming from along the creek itself, or very close by, on the lake-front."

Bert started pacing up and down the room. "If you two are right," he said, "that narrows it down a lot. There's nothing but woods along most of the creek."

"Except where Lake Road crosses it," Freddie pointed out. "There's a row of cottages on the other side of the bridge."

Nan grabbed a pad and pencil. "Cottages," she repeated. "What else?"

Flossie stared at the ceiling and tried to think. "Well, there's the marina," she said. "That faces both the lake and the creek. And across the creek from the marina is the golf course. That's all I can think of."

"You're forgetting one thing," Bert said with a laugh. "What about the Bobbsey Lumberyard?"

"Oh, sure," said Flossie. "But the lumberyard is farther down the lake. I wasn't counting that."

"The lumberyard?" Freddie exclaimed. "Hold on!"

He ran downstairs, with his brother and sisters right behind him. Freddie grabbed one of Flossie's stained sneakers from the laundry room and held it near his nose. "I just remembered where I smelled that gunk before," he said.

"Sure," Flossie said. "Yesterday, on Chief."

Freddie gave her an exasperated look. "No,

before that! It was a couple of weeks ago, when I went down to the lumberyard with Dad. One of the guys was dipping some fence posts in a big barrel of black gunk."

He waved the sneaker in the air. "And it smelled just like this!"

9

Trapped!

Flossie stared at her brothers and sister. Was their own father's lumberyard responsible for polluting Casper Creek?

"I don't believe it!" she cried. "Daddy would never let anything bad get into the lake—would he?"

Bert looked away. "We'd better check," he said. "Dad's at the lumberyard this afternoon. As soon as Flossie gets dressed, we can ride over on our bikes and ask him what this black gunk is."

Near tears, Flossie dashed up to her room. She threw on a T-shirt and jeans, then ran back downstairs. "You'll see," she told the others, as they were getting their bikes out of the garage. "Wherever that stuff came from, it wasn't from our lumberyard."

"I hope you're right," said Nan. "But we all know Dad wouldn't let anything poisonous get into the lake on purpose."

The twins made the trip to the lumberyard in record time. Mr. Bobbsey looked surprised to see them burst into his office. As soon as they told him why they had come, though, his face grew serious.

"Fence posts?" he repeated. "It sounds as if you're talking about creosote. That's a kind of tar that's used to keep wood from rotting when it gets wet a lot. Come with me."

He led the twins to the far side of the lumberyard, near the lakefront. Then he unlocked the door of a small metal building. "Here's where we keep any chemicals that are harmful or might catch fire," he explained.

"We don't want them anywhere near the lumber sheds, of course."

Flossie noticed a shallow concrete gutter that went all around the building. "Daddy?" she asked. "What's that for?"

"Well, Flossie, the building is sealed pretty tightly," he replied. "But if some of the containers of chemicals *did* break somehow, whatever was inside might leak out. This gutter would catch the harmful chemicals before they got into the ground. Then they couldn't damage our water supply. It's important to think ahead, before some accident harms the environment."

Inside, Mr. Bobbsey took the twins over to a stack of big metal barrels. "These hold the creosote," he said, pointing to the barrels. "The containers are sealed, but you can still get a whiff."

Freddie leaned closer and took a deep breath. "That's it," he said, starting to cough. "But how did it get into Casper Creek?"

"Not from our lumberyard," Mr. Bobbsey

said firmly. "You have my word on that. If there's any creosote left over when we finish one of these barrels, we seal it up. Then we have it trucked to a special dump. That lake out there is mighty important to all of us in Lakeport. We're not going to take any chances of harming it."

Flossie was glad to leave the warehouse. The smells inside were starting to make her feel dizzy.

"Would you like to look at the area where we treat the lumber?" Mr. Bobbsey asked. "It's an interesting process."

"Sure," Bert replied. He and Nan followed their father as he made his way between two tall stacks of lumber.

"Come on," Freddie said, tugging at Flossie's sleeve.

"Just a sec," Flossie replied, staring along the shore of the lake. "Look over there, at the marina. They must be building a new dock."

Freddie shrugged. "So what?"

Flossie narrowed her eyes. "See those logs sticking out of the water, and that stack of them on the bank?" she said. "Don't they look awfully dark, like they were painted with something?"

"Creosote!" Freddie exclaimed. "That's where it came from! We've solved the mystery!"

"We'll have to check it out before we can say anything," Flossie warned. "I bet we can get past the fence if we go down by the water."

The twins hurried down to the edge of the lake and walked along the old wharf. Long ago, sailing ships had brought deckloads of lumber to the wharf. Now it wasn't used at all. The twins reached the end of the wharf and swung down. They then crawled under the chain-link fence.

Sunday afternoon was a busy time at the Lakeport Marina. None of the boaters took any notice of two more kids wandering around. Flossie and Freddie went over to the stack of pilings. They didn't have to get too close. They could smell the creosote from six feet away.

"Look at that drum," Freddie said in disgust. "The cover isn't even on tight. Don't these people have any brains?"

"But we still don't know how the creosote is getting into the creek," Flossie said. "Let's take a look around on that side of the marina."

The twins walked along the path that led past the docks. Then Flossie saw a man coming toward them. He looked familiar. He noticed them, too. A puzzled look crossed his face. After they passed him, Flossie remembered. He was the man whose paintbrush Chief had tried to take.

"We'd better hurry," Flossie told Freddie in a low voice.

They reached the end of the path. Then they turned past a shed where boats were stored in winter. From behind them, someone shouted, "Hey! Where are you kids going?"

"Run!" Freddie said.

The area on the other side of the shed, near

the edge of Casper Creek, was a maze of old boats. Some were propped up on timbers. Others were leaning crazily to one side. The Bobbseys dodged around them, first one way, then another.

"We've got to hide!" Flossie gasped. She looked around. Not too far away, on the bank of the creek, was a rickety wooden shack. The door was slightly open.

"In there," Freddie said. "Come on!"

The twins dashed across the open space to the shack and darted inside. Freddie shoved the door closed behind them.

"Phew!" said Flossie. "We're safe!"

"Not exactly," Freddie said in a worried voice. He held out his hand. "Look."

Flossie looked. Freddie was holding a door-knob.

"It came off," he said. "That means we're trapped in here. And I'm sure I smell creosote —lots of it."

Flossie glanced around. The shack was so rickety that sunlight came in through the cracks between the boards. There was only one small, cobweb-covered window. It was high up in the back wall.

Freddie walked over to take a closer look. But as he reached the wall, his foot banged into a big metal can. It turned over with a thud. A black gooey liquid started to ooze out. Both he and Flossie started coughing as the fumes began to fill the little shack.

10

A Promise for the Future

"We'd better get out of here," Freddie said. "I'm starting to get dizzy."

"Me, too," Flossie replied. "But how?"

Freddie looked at his twin. "If I give you a boost, could you get out that window?"

"It's awfully high and small," she said. "But I'll try."

Freddie put his back against the wall and cupped his hands. Flossie climbed from his hands to his shoulders.

"I can reach the window," she called down.

"But it's stuck shut. I'm going to try to push it open."

"Just hurry," said Freddie. "I don't know if I can hold you up much longer."

Flossie started banging on the window with her fist. Freddie's shoulders were aching, and his knees were beginning to feel like rubber. Worse, he could feel another cough starting, deep down in his chest. "Hurry!" he said again, more urgently.

"I can't . . . There!"

Dust showered down on Freddie's head as the window swung open.

"I'm climbing out," Flossie called. "One, two, three—!"

Suddenly the weight lifted from Freddie's shoulders. Relieved, he took a deep breath. Then he wished he hadn't. All the coughs that followed made him double over. He staggered to the door and began to bang on it.

It seemed like forever, but finally a deep voice from outside called, "Stand back, in there!"

With a crash, the door flew open. Freddie stumbled outside and pulled in great gulps of fresh air. Finally he straightened up and looked around. He saw Flossie, with cobwebs in her hair, and Bert and Nan. His father was there, too, looking both worried and relieved. Standing beside Mr. Bobbsey was the man in the paint-stained overalls.

"Listen, I'm in charge of this place," the man said angrily. "I want to know what you kids were doing in there. That's trespassing."

Mr. Bobbsey stepped forward and glanced into the shack. "You're in charge, are you?" he said. "Would you mind telling us why you're storing dangerous chemicals in a place like this, right next to Casper Creek?"

The man shifted from one foot to the other. "I don't know what you're talking about," he said.

Flossie pulled on her father's arm. "Come see what I found, when I climbed down from that window."

She led the others to the back of the shack,

at the edge of the creek. "Look. See that shiny puddle?" she said, pointing to the ground next to the shack. "That must be stuff that leaked through the floorboards. It runs down the bank and into the water."

"There are laws against polluting streams," Freddie spoke up. "We learned all about them in science class."

The man was chewing the edge of his thumb. "Hey, it's not my fault," he said finally. "I didn't even know that junk was in there. I'm only the painter. Mr. Slade, the marina manager, quit last week and moved to Oregon. I'm just looking after things until they get a new manager."

"What are you going to do about this stuff that's poisoning our creek?" Flossie demanded.

"The new manager will take care of it," the man told her. He edged away from them. "I'll be sure to tell him about it when he comes."

"No way! That's not good enough!" Freddie cried. "Our dog could have died because of that creosote. Another dog got sick, too, from swimming in the creek. And the more chemicals that leak into Casper Creek, the harder it'll be to get the water clean again!"

"Freddie is right," Mr. Bobbsey said. "I'm sure the new manager, whoever he is, will be spending a lot of time on this problem. But it's important to start now. You should at least move all the chemicals in the shed somewhere else, away from the stream and the lakefront."

"Well, I guess I could do that," the man said slowly. "I've got a couple of men here this afternoon who could give me a hand. But I sure hope I don't get in trouble over it."

"It really is important to take care of this right away, before more poisons get into the water," Nan said.

"That's right," Bert added. "Just tell the people who own the marina that you saved them a lot of trouble by doing something as soon as you knew about the problem."

* * *

Mr. Bobbsey loaded the twins' bikes on top of the car. As they were driving home from the lumberyard, Bert said, "I had a hunch you guys might be checking out the marina. Then Nan spotted those creosote-covered pilings, and we were sure."

"But we couldn't believe it when we saw Flossie crawling out that little window," Nan added. "Next time, let us know what you're up to, okay?"

Freddie rolled his eyes. He and Flossie didn't need Bert and Nan acting like babysitters. After all, they'd just solved the mystery of Chief's sickness. And they'd done more to clean up Casper Creek than a dozen Saturdays of picking up litter.

"Daddy?" Flossie said. She leaned forward in her seat. "What'll happen now?"

"Well, I imagine the marina people will have to pay to remove the creosote and whatever else leaked into the creek from that shed," Mr. Bobbsey replied. "And there are lots of folks in Lakeport who are concerned about protecting our environment. We'll all keep an eye on the cleanup company to make sure it does a good job. We don't want anything like this to happen again."

He pulled into the driveway. The twins piled out of the car and raced for the back door. Flossie was the first one there. She rushed into the living room and flung herself down next to Chief's basket. She gave the sheepdog a big hug. He sat up, wagged his tail, and started to lick her face.

"Chief," Flossie said, wagging a finger at him. "The next time you take a swim in Casper Creek, you may get muddy and wet, but you won't get sick. And that's a promise!"

THE HARDY BOYS® SERIES By Franklin W. Dixon

- ☐ NIGHT OF THE WEREWOLF—#59
  70993 $3.50
- ☐ MYSTERY OF THE SAMURAI SWORD—#60
  67302 $3.50
- ☐ THE PENTAGON SPY—#61
  67221 $3.50
- ☐ THE APEMAN'S SECRET—#62
  69068 $3.50
- ☐ THE MUMMY CASE—#63
  64289 $3.99
- ☐ MYSTERY OF SMUGGLERS COVE—#64
  66229 $3.50
- ☐ THE STONE IDOL—#65
  69402 $3.50
- ☐ THE VANISHING THIEVES—#66
  63890 $3.50
- ☐ THE OUTLAW'S SILVER—#67
  64285 $3.50
- ☐ DEADLY CHASE—#68
  62477 $3.50
- ☐ THE FOUR-HEADED DRAGON—#69
  65797 $3.50
- ☐ THE INFINITY CLUE—#70
  69154 $3.50
- ☐ TRACK OF THE ZOMBIE—#71
  62623 $3.50
- ☐ THE VOODOO PLOT—#72
  64287 $3.50
- ☐ THE BILLION DOLLAR RANSOM—#73
  66228 $3.50
- ☐ TIC-TAC-TERROR—#74
  66858 $3.50
- ☐ TRAPPED AT SEA—#75
  64290 $3.50
- ☐ GAME PLAN FOR DISASTER—#76
  72321 $3.50
- ☐ THE CRIMSON FLAME—#77
  64286 $3.50
- ☐ CAVE IN—#78
  69486 $3.50
- ☐ SKY SABOTAGE—#79
  62625 $3.50
- ☐ THE ROARING RIVER MYSTERY—#80
  73004 $3.50
- ☐ THE DEMON'S DEN—#81
  62622 $3.50
- ☐ THE BLACKWING PUZZLE—#82
  70472 $3.50
- ☐ THE SWAMP MONSTER—#83
  49727 $3.50
- ☐ REVENGE OF THE DESERT PHANTOM—#84
  49729 $3.50

- ☐ SKYFIRE PUZZLE—#85
  67458 $3.50
- ☐ THE MYSTERY OF THE SILVER STAR—#86
  64374 $3.50
- ☐ PROGRAM FOR DESTRUCTION—#87
  64895 $3.50
- ☐ TRICKY BUSINESS—#88
  64973 $3.50
- ☐ THE SKY BLUE FRAME—#89
  64974 $3.50
- ☐ DANGER ON THE DIAMOND—#90
  63425 $3.99
- ☐ SHIELD OF FEAR—#91
  66308 $3.50
- ☐ THE SHADOW KILLERS—#92
  66309 $3.50
- ☐ THE BILLION DOLLAR RANSOM—#93
  66228 $3.50
- ☐ BREAKDOWN IN AXEBLADE—#94
  66311 $3.50
- ☐ DANGER ON THE AIR—#95
  66305 $3.50
- ☐ WIPEOUT—#96
  66306 $3.50
- ☐ CAST OF CRIMINALS—#97
  66307 $3.50
- ☐ SPARK OF SUSPICION—#98
  66304 $3.50
- ☐ DUNGEON OF DOOM—#99
  69449 $3.50
- ☐ THE SECRET OF ISLAND TREASURE—#100
  69450 $3.50
- ☐ THE MONEY HUNT—#101
  69451 $3.50
- ☐ TERMINAL SHOCK—#102
  69288 $3.50
- ☐ THE MILLION-DOLLAR NIGHTMARE—#103
  69272 $3.50
- ☐ TRICKS OF THE TRADE—#104
  69273 $3.50
- ☐ THE SMOKE SCREEN MYSTERY—#105
  69274 $3.50
- ☐ ATTACK OF THE VIDEO VILLIANS—#106
  69275 $3.50
- ☐ PANIC ON GULL ISLAND—#107
  69276 $3.50
- ☐ FEAR ON WHEELS—#108
  69277 $3.50
- ☐ THE PRIME-TIME CRIME—#109
  69278 $3.50
- ☐ THE SECRET OF SIGMA SEVEN—#110
  72717 $3.50
- ☐ THE HARDY BOYS® GHOST STORIES
  69133 $3.50

NANCY DREW® and THE HARDY BOYS® are
trademarks of Simon & Schuster, registered in the United States Patent and Trademark Office.

AND DON'T FORGET...NANCY DREW CASEFILES® NOW AVAILABLE IN PAPERBACK.

Simon & Schuster, Mail Order Dept. HB5
200 Old Tappan Road, Old Tappan, NJ 07675
Please send me copies of the books checked. Please add appropriate local sales tax.

☐ Enclosed full amount per copy with this coupon (Send
check or money order only.)
Please be sure to include proper postage and handling:
95¢—first copy
50¢—each additonal copy ordered.

☐ If order is for $10.00 or more, you
may charge to one of the following
accounts:
☐ Mastercard   ☐ Visa

Name _____   Credit Card No. _____

Address _____

City _____   Card Expiration Date _____

State _____ Zip _____   Signature _____

Books listed are also available at your local bookstore. Prices are subject to change without notice.   HBD-41